Snapdragons & Seductions

A Wild Blooms and TeXan Devils crossover

SOFIA AVES

SOFIA AVES

COPYRIGHT © SOFIA AVES 2023

First Edition

Published by Little Quail Press

Cover Design by Opium House

Editing by Partners in Crime

ISBN: 978-1-922448-57-6

CONTENTS

Acton Cunningham never played into the political side of policing, until he's recruited for Austin's Texas Ranger Special Unit.

Floss Buchannan loves being a florist. But pretending to be a Ranger's fiancé wasn't in her future until Acton Cunningham walked into her posy of snapdragons…

AUTHOR NOTE

Welcome to the shared world of *Wild Blooms*. Drawn together by a love of romance, we have written a series of stories linked by a single phone call that changes the course of our character's lives-for the better, of course. It also gives insight into the types of stories each of us love to write…and sometimes a glimpse into our worlds.

Snapdragons & Seductions is linked to my TeXan Devils world set in Austin, Texas. My heart always lies with romantic suspense, though for Acton, my fledgling Texas ranger, a decent dose of crazy love seemed apt. In his and Floss' book, another couple feature on the sidelines, backing their friends (as they should!). Andy and Ella have their own sweet second chance romance and this story continues on after their Happily Ever After (and of all my books, theirs is one of my absolute favorites).

I hope you enjoy my ego-hopeful Ranger finding his feet and the girl he can't get out of his heart.

Sofia xx

For everyone who has a dream but is scared to start something…

Try.

Make something magical.

Even if it's a swamp unicorn with trash panda ears.

"Thank you for calling Cygnature Blooms where bigger is always better, this is Tee. We specialize in healing hearts worldwide. May I have your location, please?"

"Austin, Texas."

"Thank you. I'll direct your call."

CHAPTER ONE

ACTON

I stood in front of the bow windows of Wild Flowers, the local branch Cygnature Blooms had directed me to for Austin, Texas. I adjusted my white hat with one hand, the mass of color a sensory overload for a poor farm boy-cum-law enforcement officer who recently received the career upgrade of a lifetime.

My heart thrummed in my chest as I grabbed a posy of flowers from a bucket and crossed the threshold my best friend and co-Texas Ranger Andy Matthews had directed me to, citing glowing reviews for the small florist shop around the corner from Ranger HQ in Austin, Texas. Now that we worked shoulder to shoulder, Andy's comments railed my ears frequently as talked up the service every chance he got.

He should; his wife owned the place.

"Hi, I have a—" A bell jingled merrily as the door swung open and back too fast. I pressed a hand to the pristine glass, leaving a full hand print on it to avoid face planting on the thing. "A pick up for—" The door slammed shut, the bell dinging my arrival in a grand gesture as I talked to an empty shop. "—Cunningham. Hello?"

I edged into the shop, my posy dropping by my side, staring at the array of color that filled the small shop to overflowing, giving what could have been a clean, open space a cluttered look, like a flower jungle. The flowers stared back at me with their single, unblinking eye.

"Welcome to Wild Blooms," one said in a distinctly feminine voice.

"Ah, hi?" I walked deeper into the shop and stopped at a bunch of daisies that appeared to want to hold a conversation.

Clearly, my initiation into the local Texas Ranger unit had gone to my head.

Or maybe it was the plethora of floral scents that permeated the air in a cloying cloud.

"Can I help you?" asked a crimson dahlia.

I stared in bemusement as the flower wiggled, leaning forward in its display. A pair of bright blue eyes edged in sunshine gold rose over the top. Messy, beach babe blonde hair attached to a heart shaped face waved above the flower, and I adjusted my focal point to the ruby red lips that smiled as I swallowed hard. The color of her lipstick matched the dahlia the woman crouched behind.

"I have an order for Cunningham to pick up. And these, please." I waved my posy in the air a little too vigorously, relieved my voice didn't break.

A petal floated between me and Miss Dahlia, who rose to her full height of not at all tall, reaching about mid-chest on me.

Because that's how we measure height. By where a woman comes up to on your body.

I shushed the snarky little voice in my brain that sounded a little too much like the best friend who could have been an older brother to me. Andy stood beside me at the small ceremony a week prior that included me into his unit's ranks with his usual easy grin and a few practical jokes on the side. Nothing out of the usual.

But the nerves on standing on that dias while Rhys Archer pinned a shiny star to my chest and offered me a white hat had nothing on encountering dahlia-girl.

Initiation is most definitely not the hardest part of my week, not the pinnacle.

"Sure." She thrust the dahlia into my hands, extricating herself from a tangle of strangling orchids determined to mummify her in a swath of green, reaching vines. "Hold Dolly."

"Hell." I plopped the potted plant that seemed out of place in a florist shop onto a stand and placed my posy on top. "Let's get you out of that mess. Wait, who's Dolly?" I

3

scanned our surrounds for a small dog or maybe a cat, but came up blank.

"Careful, don't break anything," she warned, wiggling two free fingers as greenery encased her.

Untangling the vines took up most of my brain capacity for the next few minutes. "I swear this thing is actively growing," I muttered, tugging the last knotted leaves apart with pizzazz. And a snap. I looked at the tiny piece of orchid that looked like it began to wilt sadly before my eyes. "Ah—" I tugged at it and realized it was attached to a much longer stem. "Damn."

"And here I thought Texas Rangers did not swear." Dahlia girl put one hand on her hip, concealing her smile badly. "Where's Dolly?"

"Um…" I looked around for a pet again but couldn't see anything. "Dolly is a…butterfly?"

She laughed at me, the sound tinkling in a choir of bells that broadened the space around us and zoned me out to everything but her all at once. "No, silly. Dolly the Dahlia. She's my house plant. You're the new Ranger Andy mentioned, aren't you?"

She plucked the plant from my inert fingers that I offered, changing tack at something akin to lightspeed.

"Yeah."

Yeah? That's the best we've got?

I blinked and said nothing else.

Apparently so.

I bit back a groan as Miss Dahlia and Dolly watched on, bemusement curling lips and petals of the same share.

…And now we're talking to plants. Excellent progress, Cunningham.

"Awesome. I also have a package for you?" She smiled brightly, though her fingers tightened around Dolly's bright yellow pot. Tiny pink petals decorated the sides in a cascade of spring.

"Yeah." My mouth dried up. "Yes, and these please." I recovered enough of my manners to wave my posy about. "Sorry about the orchid."

"Totally forgive because you know what an orchid is," she said in a serious tone. Something sparkled in the depths of her blue eyes.

I tipped my head to one side. "You're not Texan born, are you?"

"Ohhh, the Ranger is out in force today," she chimed, heading toward the back of the store. "Was it my non-existent accent that gave it away?"

No. Your sense of humor is a bit screwy for this state is all. I managed to hold that thought in. "Could be some of your speech."

"But it's not, is it?" She grinned at me, almost buoyant as she chatted away, grabbing a card and reading details aloud. "Acton Cunningham, newest Texas ranger and…ohhh." She pressed both lips together, her shoulders shaking. Her face turned a bright shade of pink, almost the same color as Dolly's bloom.

"And?" I prompted, managing to keep a straight face.

"Ah, you and Andy are friends, right?" She closed both eyes and peeked at me from one. "Not…you get along, huh?"

I watched her try to suppress whatever the hell my clearly ex-best friend had written on the note for the flowers I was meant to drop over to his aunt's for organizing a tiramisu slab cake for my swearing in ceremony. Yes, she spoke differently. Her sense of humor was a bit skewed. But that wasn't quite it… I took in the tanned arms, the sun bleached hair that bobbed around her face in dirty blonde tangled waves like she'd just gotten out of the…

"California. South of LA?"

She blinked. Her mouth relaxed, her color coming back to its normal tanned hue as she beamed at me. "Yes! Huntington Beach. Born and bred." Her eyes twinkled, and in a moment I could see her walking along the beach in a bikini, a sarong wrapped around her waist, beachy blonde locks blowing messily in the breeze in a perfect meld of easy going attitude and wild child.

Or maybe *flower child.*

Then her words registered, and I remembered her odd sense of humor.

"Was that a bread joke?" I asked warily, watching Dolly as she bobbed about with— "I don't know your name."

"Floss Buchanan. Ella hired me last month to help out with opening the shop and getting stock sorted plus a few other things. She wanted live flowers and while Ella can make arrangements like nothing else, her thumb is…what's the opposite of green?"

"Black?" I offered, then cringed. "Damn. I am an asshole today."

Floss Buchanan—her name rolled through my mind in a little wave of its own—nodded enthusiastically. "Yep! Sure you are. But that's okay, newest Ranger. We all have off days. How's Andy?"

I stared at her, my tongue twisted by trying to answer three questions at once. "Uh, he's good, I'm sure. Wait. Why do you ask?"

"Because he—um…" Floss turned Dolly pink again and sighed. "Well, see for yourself." She swiveled the screen around on its stand so I could read the notes for my order.

Acton Cunningham, newest Texas Ranger and ultimate virgin. Needs a good spanking and a great night to imbibe some fun times into his serious nature. Floss, take note.

"Jesus." I swiped a hand over my face, knocking my hat to the floor. From the heat emanating from my skin, I guessed *Dolly pink* was the order of the day. "I'm so—"

Floss pealed into laughter, clutching my order in its box. "He's such a charmer, isn't he? I'm more of *a-thinker-and-a-lover* girl than a *joker and a fun times* girl. But either way is probably fun." Shwe smiled and her lips twitched as she watched me, not handing over the parcel.

Okey-dokey. Here we go.

I picked up my hat and left my ego on the floor. "Yes, I'm the newest Texas Ranger, not that it will hold if I kill my best friend anytime soon." I grinned to let her know I was joking as her eyes widened the slightest amount. *God, she's breathtaking.* "I take myself way too seriously, so Andy's right on that account. Not a virgin, so sorry about that but not a man slut either. And I'll leave the spankings to others, thanks. I don't mind a bit of spice in my sex life but skin to skin is more the level for me." I stopped talking and the shop fell totally and utterly silent.

Floss stared at me, her humor faded, replaced with a brand new sheen of pink that might have been embarrassment incarnate, but came closer to…

Did I just turn my little florist on?

I smirked, reaching for my package and placed my posy on top. "You take credit, right?"

Floss nodded, her top teeth sinking slowly into her bottom lip that pillowed around the nip.

My pants tightened as I imagined her lips stretched wide around my cock and—

Get your shit together, Cunningham, or Andy's prediction of spanking will be true in another sense.

Right as he walked me out the door of Ranger HQ, which was conveniently located around the corner. Nothing like having your ass handed to you on day five of employment, with the bonus round of screwing your career to the floor in the process.

I swiped my card, studying Floss Buchanan as she flitted around the desk, repositioning my parcel and Dolly several times. An idea began to form inside my mind—cute and cowardly all at once. *Hear me roar.*

The machine beeped, letting me know my payment had gone through. Floss pushed my box across the counter, still nibbling on her bottom lip where it turned pinker and pinker.

Sucking in a deep breath, I grabbed my goods and spat out the thought before it had finished forming in full— never a good idea. "How would you like to date a Ranger?"

"Would I what?" Her lip popped free as she stared at me. "Did you just say—" her entire face suffused with a cute flush that did nothing to ease my state of arousal.

9

I held my box a little lower. "A Ranger has a semi-political position, which makes it being a little different from the position a local cop holds. I need to look like a family man, and I'd love to have someone like you standing beside me at events. What do you say?"

"Say?" her mouth dropped open. "I'd say that's a pretty sexist and egotistical statement."

I grinned. *Girl's got balls.* I liked that. A lot. "Then you'll love this. Don't get attached. It's a friend offer, not a romantic one. You're cute as a button, a little different, and well spoken. I'm a guy in a desperate need of…"

"Arm candy? A—" she mumbled something under her breath that sounded a lot like *a knee to the groin.*

"Never said I was a romantic. And I'm struggling with a lot of things." Mostly my own ego and where in the hell I sat in my new world at this point.

"I can tell." Floss narrowed her eyes. "Let me get this right. You want me to be a pretend girlfriend and go to events with you. And…dates? What are the boundaries of this little scam of yours?"

"No scam." My grin strained at the edges. "Just a desperate man asking—begging?—for help." I knew my words did not paint me in a solid light, but it was what came out and I was going with it. "Can I bribe you with dinner under the stars? Favorite movie?"

She snorted. "You *are* desperate."

"Do it." A high voice hissed from a back room.

I stared behind Floss. "Do you hide your conscience out there?"

She sighed. "Only my boss." Her lips pursed though her lips curved up at the corners, highlighting high cheekbones as she stared me down. "All right. I'll do it."

I could have whooped and done a jig, but I managed to doff my hat and collect my packages. "Thank you, ma'm."

"Don't you *ma'am* me," she warned, her mouth pursed in a cute little rosette. "Do you need my number?"

"I'll fix that!" the disembodied voice out the back squeaked.

Andy's wife. Ella.

It had to be.

I grinned, finding Floss' eyes with mine and holding her there in a silent communication of promises and sweet things. A blush rose in her cheeks, her lips parting on a soft breath.

"Good to meet you, Floss." I nodded toward the open door of their office room. "Ella."

Two voices bid me a soft goodbye as I left the florist shop, half happy to have the issue of the much needed wife/girlfriend situation handled according to the world of

Andy, and half wondering what the hell I'd just let myself in for.

Both of us.

A message beeped in my pocket on cue—either Andy telling me I'd hashed it up with some appropriate gif, or his wife giving me hell and Floss' details, assuming the girl agreed to my plan. Which was more of an outline than anything else. I'd managed to get into the Rangers unit after a whole lot of hard work. Surely managing one girl for a short period wouldn't be that hard.

CHAPTER TWO

FLOSS

"Can you believe that man?" I blinked as I rotated on my heel to face the empty office doorway. A doorway that remained empty as I stared at it. "Ella? You can come out now."

Ella, my boss and best friend in the world, squealed as she darted out of the office from where she'd obviously been hiding just beyond the door frame. "I'm so excited for you! Andy told me all about him. He's a brand new ranger, hot to trot, keen as burger mustard and gorgeous to boot. Plus, he's single and wants to make all the best impressions! You can't lose," she told me seriously, then squeaked again. "Girl, I'm so happy for you!"

"Whoa. Hold that race horse." I held up both hands. "And who calls it *burger mustard*? Did you hear the crap that man spouted?"

Ella nodded enthusiastically. "Yup. You got this one spinning good. Must be all those SoCal vibes."

13

"Mhmm." I didn't correct my friend on Californian locations as I had bigger issues to argue over right now. "So you *want* me to go out with him? Mister...Cunningham?" Never mind the fact that I'd been so busy staring at his movie star worthy chiseled jawline or the way those shoulders filled out his shirt. I'd always been a sucker for a good set of shoulders, and they'd always gotten me in trouble. The sky blue eyes that stared back beneath a cute swath of sandy brown-blond hair didn't help either.

Damnit, shoulders and blue eyes. I'm screwed.

Ella, pursed her lips, a hand pressed to her swollen belly as she bowed forward. "Man, I'm lucky I could get off the floor."

"I reckon so." I eyed her swollen body critically. "Should you even be working? Maybe you should go home and rest or do the books or do Andy... Or something."

"Probably." Ella puffed part of a laugh. "Though I'm not sure sex would even work right now. Will you be all right on your own?"

I smiled and nodded. "Today's orders are already packed and I started on tomorrow this morning so I know what we need to order. Plus, I've got the office to look after." I'd started splitting and repotting some of my own orchids during quiet hours in the shop, all wrapped up with a bright red or white ribbon around their pot. "I'll be fine. Besides, I have Dolly to look after me."

Ella rolls her eyes. "That damn Dahlia..."

"I know." I smirked. "Anyway, I think I gave a Texas Ranger a bit of a run for his money."

Ella nodded, her gaze flitting to the door. "Never in doubt. Call me if you need anything."

"We'll be fine." I shooed Ella out the door, not looking when the little bell above it jingled twice in quick succession. I sighed. "What did you forget?"

"I've got a delivery for a D-duffy? Duffrey. No, Godfrey? This writing is so bad." Out of the corner of my eye I saw a white and orange blur. I straightened to find a lady with frizzy orange hair who attempted to push the mass back from her red, sweaty face staring at me, holding a small stack of boxes.

"Oh hell. I'm so sorry. I thought you were my boss. "

"I wish. You got a Goffrey here?" She offered the boxes to me and passed a small tablet to sign along one edge of the box.

I shook my head. "Wrong address. Sorry." I checked the boxes and frowned. "Well, right address, wrong name." Maybe it was a supplier of Ella's who'd gotten the name wrong? I checked over the boxes and the paperwork but couldn't find anything on the computer, and there were no other markings. I shook my head again. "Sorry. Try the shops on either side?" I indicated to the neighboring coffee shop and shoe shops that flanked us on the streetfront.

The driver shook her head, hefting her burden back to the front doors. I held it for her as she looked at both in both directions and turned left with a shrug.

I made it back to the front desk as my phone beeped. Pulling it out of my apron, I checked the messages. It was from Ella, but she hadn't said much, just a phone number.

Acton Cunningham.

Pressing my lips together to hold back a sigh, I tossed my phone onto the counter and ignored it throughout the afternoon, repotting my orchids and working on my bow tying skills. More than once Ella suggested I go to bow tying school. Hours of well tied bows later, the shop was filled with red and white.

I wandered about, adjusting my earlier work before my skills improved. I could see which were the most recent, and fixed the wilting ones. Finally, I managed to get back to Dolly and checked my phone. I shunted the dahlia to one side, checking her leaves and giving her a spritz of cool water. A few messages sat waiting on my phone, one with a new number that I didn't recognise, though it matched the one Ella sent across earlier.

Way too much pressure for a single girl. Though the man clearly had skills, though they weren't in the dating department. That made him kind of…endearing. I snorted at the thought, bending over the counter to stretch my back while I scrolled through them.

Acton Cunningham sent through a note about a dinner date, another about an upcoming event, and questions about my favorite flowers. The man was a chatterbox, if not in person. I wanted to be able to tell him that he had settled into the new Ranger unit he'd been assigned to; nothing could be more obvious that the job was his calling; it was his confidence that failed him.

He mentioned that, being a new Ranger, though thanks to Andy and Ella's general gossip, I knew plenty about the new onboarding Ranger. He compared himself to his friend, Andy Mathews; tall, straightlaced straight down the line, romantic, and was the most loyal and steadfast Ranger I've ever met. And being the best friend and employee of his wife, I'd met quite a few.

From what I'd seen, the Rangers in Andy's unit had a lot in common. Usually, they were quiet men, no show ponying, and always honest with a warm smile. Except Jake, but the pale blond Ranger fell into a cheeky league of his own. Apart, they were solitary figures; together, they created a band of brothers who backed each other at every turn, even if they didn't always agree with each other.

Acton Cunningham was a bit like all of them, and nothing like anyone else I'd ever met. His looks could place him in Hollywood but…I didn't think that sort of spotlight was his aim, despite his epic outgoing personality. No, I suspected the newest Ranger hadn't found a place in the world just yet.

The doorbell tinkled again. I raised my head, though I was still re-reading Acton's messages; poor form in the shop and I knew it. Ella would have my head.

"Hi, welcome to—" I lifted my head and came face-to-face with the man himself. "Acton. Hi." I stared into those blue eyes, then my attention waned, captivated by those shoulders hidden beneath his shirt–who wouldn't perv on a single Texas Ranger if given the chance? *Get a grip on yourself, Floss.* My breath fluttered a little. I blamed it on the Socal girl in me, then shook myself internally, gripping one of Dolly's deep green leaves for moral support. This was going all the wrong places fast. "Don't you have a job to do?"

That's what chose to come out? I closed my eyes. *Brilliant.*

Acton answered me with a half smile. "Is it wrong that I want to come in and say hi?"

I raised both my eyebrows. "On the first week in your new job, on a work day?"

His smile grew a little more carefree, almost…reckless. "And seeing as that's across the street from you… I'm on coffee duty as a junior and that's right next door. I said I'd be ten or fifteen minutes and wanted to plan something with you." He wiggled his eyebrows and slid a look at Dolly.

I stifled a giggle. "She's not going to come out of the corner and attack you."

"Uh huh," he murmured. "Are you doing anything tonight?"

"Tonight?" *He moves fast.* "Probably sleeping. On my own," I amended.

"That's a good thing," he said seriously. "I didn't ask you if you had a significant other."

"I don't." My lips pressed together to keep from laughing. "You're really awkward at this thing, you know that right?"

"Must be why I'm single."

"Well, you're not now." I booped his nose with an orchid sprig. Acton went cross-eyed, and I winced. "Please don't do that. Okay. You said you needed a girlfriend, and you needed to be presentable. I'm a California beach girl, and prim and proper is not me. At all."

I had nothing holding me in one place. No family, no home loan. I couch surfed at friend's places for the better part of my teens when I couldn't afford accommodation on top of college fees. Not that I did anything with my business management accolades, working as an assistant Ella's the florist shop, but I loved my job and I loved my life.

Nothing Mister Cunningham had to say about that date of his would change who I was.

"No, you're not." A small smile curved upwards. "But you are stunning. Do I need any other reason?"

"Why not ask me out for real then?" I asked before the thought filled out in my mind. "I'm sorry, I —"

"Because there's less chance of rejection when it's not real. It won't hurt as much." Straightening, Acton still smiled at me, that incessant but seriously cute smile, and I realized just how tall he was.

"What are you, six and a half feet tall? Seven?" I raised up on my toes to measure my eyeline against his chest. I came up to around nipple height, apparently.

"You're short, I'm tall. Not much else to it, Floss." He stared down at me with darkening eyes.

My stomach clenched against the flash of desire that flickered in his gaze when he said my name, and I tried to brush it off nonchalantly. "For a Ranger, I guess." Andy would be of a height with him, maybe a little shorter than Acton. "So…how are you dealing with this dating thing? Are you still nervous as hell?"

He shrugged. "I've got trust issues. A broken heart takes a long time to heal, apparently. But…I'm willing to be a student, if you're willing to teach me."

I held my breath for a short period, the olive branch extended between us, and nodded. "I'll do my best. But I can't promise results," I warned.

"Noted." Acton glanced around at the shop. "You… redecorated?"

I laughed. "Yes, I was on a bow theme today. And I repotted and split some of the orchids for a bigger display."

"That sounds fun."

I smiled. "I love having my hands in the dirt."

Acton's lips twisted, and I swore to myself that if the next words out of his mouth were *dirty girl*, I'd slap him with Dolly's petals.

"What about you? What are you working on for your first week?"

"There's an upshoot of drugs in the area. Apparently previous investigations knocked out the bigger dealers and suppliers, for whatever reason. We're not seeing what's coming through in the usual channels in the usual way. And it's local. Last night, the girls next door in the coffee shop found a local out the back, overdosed. She went to the hospital, and looks like she'll be okay, but still..." His lips pressed into a hard line

"I hope you work it out." I leaned forward, watching him become animated with his talk of his work. It was the first time I'd had a glimpse into who Acton Cunningham really was.

And I liked it.

"The oddest thing is, the girl who OD'd... she'd never done drugs before. Family says she's not a user, the best friend, even her ex-boyfriend agrees. And she doesn't know how they got into her system, especially by something that should've been injected, or internally taken."

"The coffee shop girls must have been shocked to find her there."

"I know the situation bothers Andy more than he lets on. Somebody on the outside of some social circle frequently gets hurt when drug channels get loose, and there's little we can do about it unless we get to the source of the problem faster. This one... Neither of us have any idea how the drug is being trafficked into Austin. Help me. You're down here on the street level. Maybe you'll see something we don't?"

I shrugged hopelessly."I can try. We've had odd boxes and a confused delivery driver, but that's about all." Searching for drugs was so far out of my frame of reference, I wasn't sure how much help I could be. The most I'd seen of drugs in my life was smoking pot at a friend's place after a party one night. I hated the way it made me feel, and I'd never done it again.

His phone beeped. "Well, my time's up, girls. Floss. Dolly." He doffed his hat to us, both me and the flower, that small smile curling his lips again as his gaze swept over me.

My skin zinged beneath his study, something heady developing between us in a short period of time. He stepped forward, catching my chin between his fingertips and brushed his lips over mine in a barely there kiss. My breath stalled, the world spinning too fast around me as he drew back, that same flare of desire evident in his eyes as he nodded once more.

I didn't start breathing again until Acton left the shop and I was alone with Dolly.

For the rest of my afternoon, I made up orders and completed my sweep of the store as best I could, but I couldn't help glancing over towards the Rangers HQ across the road from the shop.

But no matter how many hours I watched his office door, I didn't see Acton again that day.

CHAPTER THREE

ACTON

"Oh look. Here comes Acton Man," Jake called across the office, raising a few heads as I worked my way into the office door, my arms laden with full trays.

Ethan shook his head, ignoring the rest of the catcalls around the room as I delivered the coffee run for the day. It appeared to be Rhys Archer's way of inducting new members to the unit: start at the bottom and work your way up. Humility hurt, and I hoped to hell my stint didn't last long.

Forcing a smile on my face, I delivered Jake's coffee and flipped him off with my other hand. "Get some new lines, man. That one's had its day."

Andy laughed at his adjacent desk. "How's things going with Floss?"

"Ah—" I swallowed hard, remembering that kiss, and tried not to let the wave of arousal at the thought of her take solid form inside my slacks. "She's good."

"Mmhm." Jake muttered. "That good, huh?"

I ignored him. "How's the investigation going?"

"'Bout as good as Floss." Andy stretched his arm over his head. "Lot of loose ends, a lot of mangled ends and a shit ton of knotty bits. Sum it up?"

"Pretty well." I remembered what Floss mentioned about the packages in the shop. "Did Ella mention that they've had some odd deliveries of their own at the flower shop?"

"Florist, dickwad. Grow some culture." Jake added into the conversation like a Shakesperan aside.

"Is he always this cranky?" I threw a thumb over my shoulder raising my eyebrows at Andy.

"Nah. Probably not getting any at home."

"Fuck off," Jake grumbled. "I've got undercover to do again."

"Ah, so you won't be getting any at home, because you won't be there. Much better." Andy gave his friend a wide grin.

A knot tugged inside my heart. I'd known Andy for a hell of a long time, and had plenty of good banerting moments with him, but here in the office it was like I was the toddler swimming out to the deep end, sans floating device.

Jake swiped his coffee off the desktop, scowling at both of us, and strode from the office. The doors whooshed closed behind him, letting in a blast of too-warm air from the outside into the chilly air conditioned space.

Andy propped his elbows on the table and leaned forward. "Man, have you thought about not trying so damn hard? I mean, it's just sad." He gave me an easy grin but the concern etched in his eyes bothered me on a deep level.

I stared at him for a moment, and forced a smile on my face. "Did you just call me a wanker?"

Behind me, Ethan snorted.

"Maybe." Andy raised a shoulder, and leaned back into his chair. "Maybe a year ago I was in your position, out of my league and showing it."

"He was," Ethan muttered not so discreetly.

Andy grunted. "And now… I'm a fixture. Give it time, man. You're a fucking good cop. You'll be a better Ranger. Just let up on the trying bit. Be you and work hard. That's all it takes."

"That's it, huh?" My fake smile plastered to my face, I remembered hamming it up for Floss and Ella, trying to channel Jake prancing about the office. "Maybe y'all don't want to see my grumpy ass morning face. Don't say I didn't warn you." I cocked an eyebrow in Andy's direction and waited for Ethan's snide comment.

The office fell silent.

Andy considered me. "Pull up a chair. Let's go over this drug scheme. And I want to talk to you about Floss."

"Yeah, that didn't go so well." I ran a hand over my hair. I'd kissed her, and she said nothing, though she'd reminded me how awkward I was earlier. That stung my pride at a deep level, though I buried the unwanted emotion to focus on work instead. That at least I knew I was good at.

"Yeah? Cause Ella said she was taken with you. Coulnd't stop talking about how much you annoyed her."

I grimaced. "That's not such a great thing."

"Come on." Andy rose and grabbed Jake's vacant chair, swinging it around in my direction. "Are you kidding? That's a great thing. She likes you, man. Let up on the fake stuff and just be you. Now, work me through this because I'm missing something and I need a solid sounding board."

I took the proffered chair and sank into it, flicking open the paper files Archer insisted on keeping rather than digital, and started scanning the top one. Names and places fell into a neat list in my head as I digested the information, creating a mental pathway and seeing where it went. "Just call me Devil's advocate."

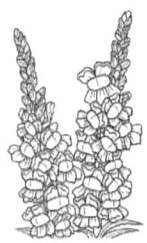

I stood in my apartment, flipping my phone over in my hand. I managed to ask Floss out on a date–albeit a fake one–which somehow felt more real than it was supposed to be when I first suggested the idea on a whim. I shaved and changed out of my work shirt, though I left my usual boots on. A little bit scuffed, a little bit worn on the sides, but they were my comfiest pair and a man had to cling to something when he was so far out of his depth, right?

She called me out, that day the florist shop. I'd ended up messaging her with a regular twenty questions. Each one added an extra knot to my stomach, while she asked about my family, and that ended the conversation as I barely spoke to mine. The reward of a career cop: no time for a social life and opting to hide behind my caseload rather than deal with family dinners where everyone had a life partner, but nme.

And so, we drifted apart.

Which was why I had to keep things both uplifting and thankful to Floss for taking me in like a city stray. Finding no reason to hang around my apartment any longer, I left the building, checking the time to make sure I arrived early, but not too early.

The exclusive rooftop bar sat above the main street level set over the hotel. I'd done a rec mission on the place before I sent an invitation to Floss. The space was tidy, neat and the staff had let me decorate our corner that overlooked a balcony and below, the city lights.

Vines crept across the back of the area, studded with orchid blooms that created a backdrop for the white-clothed table. Tea lights decorated the corners nearest the balcony that overlooked Austin's sparkling lights. Small vines wound around the table, the dark green contrasting against the white tablecloth and the rustic wooden chairs.

I placed a small burgundy box just in front of her side of the table that offered the best view and ordered a bottle of wine. It was presumptuous, perhaps, but if nothing else I wanted to appear organized.

That's so romantic, Acton.

Maybe not, but I wanted Floss to enjoy tonight. I was going to ask her to attend a stack of events with me as I knew there are quite a few festivals and holidays coming up. Tonight was my chance to actually get to know her before life got hectic for us both. Between my investigation into the drugs and finding my feet in the unit, I hadn't had time to see her again for the last few days.

Considering what I'd be asking of her, that sat poorly with me, but I shoved thoughts of work aside. Tonight wasn't about talking shop. It was about *her*.

Keep on going like that, Acton, and you'll start to sound like you actually care.

Maybe I did care. Floss was certainly in a league of her own.

I didn't have to wait long after I arrived and paid the staff in advance. Floss tripped into the balcony room from the stairwell, peering around like she was looking for waitstaff for directions, but the only people in the room were us.

She wouldn't know it, but I'd reserved the entire rooftop bar. It cost me a week's wages, but by gods was the girl worth it. She wore an aqua blue flouncy dress that dropped low over one shoulder and settled in cascading ruffles from her hips to her knees. Tan sandals with a small heel gave her golden legs an extra little bit of lift, although she wasn't really that short by any means. She was right. I was tall, and everything-and everyone-else looked a fair way down from where I stood.

Her beachy blonde hair tumbled over her shoulders in messy waves that might have been strategically twisted and decorated, but she didn't strike me as the sort of woman who spent hours on her hair just to make it look messy at the end. No, she had a sexy mussed bed head at any hour of the day, it seemed. She smiled when she spotted me, my body reacting the moment she came close. I clasped my hands in front of my crotch, calling for the deluge of blood to head north as I smiled back, keeping our space. This was an informal dinner, right?

Then why did you put so much effort into it?

31

Floss ignored the unspoken strict rules I put up between us, closing the distance to rise up onto her toes to kiss my cheek, but she couldn't reach. I held back a laugh and closed one hand around the back of her waist, dipping my head until I pressed a kiss to her lips. The contact was as brief and as barely there as it had been in the shop, but it was enough to set my blood aflame with arousal.

So much for the rule book.

Telling the downstairs situation to get a grip, I released her and drew back. Her cheeks were as flushed as I felt and I knew I wasn't the only one flustered.

"Have a seat." *Original.* "This is for you." *Stunning conversational skills.* I pushed the little box forward. She opened her mouth as though to protest, but I cut her off before she could start. "I'm going to probably put both of us through the ringer and a whole lot of pressure in the next weeks. This is my apology in advance and my gratitude for you, taking on a raw-edged cop."

Her expression softened. I hadn't told a lie, well, I might not feel like I was completely out of my league but the fact that she'd agreed to do this for me out of the blue still stunned me.

"You need to give yourself more credit," Floss murmured, taking a little box and lifting the lid. "Oh, Acton." She stared up at me with those sapphire bright eyes flooded with emotion.

32

I couldn't get the memory out of my mind of how she sighed my name.

I want to make her do that again.

She plucked the tiny red glass dahlia studs from their pillows.

"I tried to match Dolly's shade. I mean, I tried to get something for Dolly, but they didn't have anything in her size."

The joke fell flat as Floss was still studying the earrings. "They're so beautiful. Will you help me?" She passed the studs to me and slipped her gold hoops from her ears. Tucking her hair over one shoulder, she tilted her head, baring the slope of her shoulder to me.

My breath hitched at the sight, and I cleared my throat, forcing myself to focus. "I can't say this is something I've done before, so forgive me if I don't get this right first shot."

A look of bemusement mixed with exasperation slid across her face. "Acton Cunningham. I think you're pretty much perfect."

"Yeah, tell me that again in a moment after I've given you an extra piercing."

She giggled and leaned her shoulder back, giving me better access.

My fingers trembled against her skin as I slipped the tiny silver stems into her ears, and worked the butterfly back on. The tiny glass petals reflected the candlelight, sitting perfectly against the pink stain of her cheeks. I rucked her hair around her shoulders, trying not to mess it up, but she looked sexy as hell regardless of what I did. She was wearing something I'd given her. Some part of me roared its approval at that small, simple fact.

"You're beautiful." I grazed my fingers across her cheek, trailing a caress along her neck, fascinated by the way her skin flushed pink forever I touched it.

Floss sat stock still, and I stepped back to give us both a little space.

She reached up to brush your fingers over the earrings. "Thank you. You didn't have to do this. I wouldn't offer if I didn't mind giving my time to you. Plus," her nose twitched mischievously, "I can give you a run for your money as well. You're stuck with me, too. You know that, right?"

I raised an eyebrow. "Are you going to be a hellcat for me?"

Her gaze darted up to capture mine and all the breath left my lungs in an instant.

Damn but she's stunning.

I slid my hand across the table, leaving my palm open. She paused for a moment then lay her fingers in mine, giving them a little squeeze. Her skin was smooth against my scars and work-roughened callouses, though she didn't seem to mind as I laced out fingers together, trying to ignore the zings of desire that shot through me every place we touched and failed.

"That depends." She didn't expand on the hellcat comment and I didn't push it, watching her eyes twinkle as she held my hand gently.

I lent forward, drawing her gently across the table in my grip. My heart pounded as blood rushed in my ears.

Maybe pushing blood flow north was a bad idea.

I was already drunk on the mere sight of her, heading directly for that romance I promised myself I'd sit out. Pink lips parted, soft and inviting. I tasted her briefly before , but I needed more. "Flos–" My voice caught, rough and gravelly.

One of the waitstaff cleared his throat from where he stood at my elbow, breaking my peace. Floss drew back, her cheeks stained darker than ever, her hands folded tight in her lap, the moment broken.

"Wine, sir? Would you like to try?" He opened the bottle while I tried not to glare at the man.

"It's fine, thank you."

Floss picked up the menu, hiding behind it.

I opened my mouth to ask her what she liked to eat. Naturally, what actually came out was, "Are you allergic to anything?"

Fuck me.

Her head rose as she peered at me over the top of her menu. "Do you always open conversations like that? I did wonder about that form you sent me."

It was my turn to flush. I rubbed at the back of my neck. "Yeah. Sorry about that." I shut my mouth before anything else stupid fell out.

"You don't date at all, do you?" Floss placed her menu on the table and studied me.

"Nope. Got my heart broken in high school. I haven't been able to risk it since."

"Ouch." She winced for me. "First love always hurts. Wait, I should have asked— are you gay?"

A smile to show that I wasn't a frontage. "No. Should I have asked the same thing of you?"

"Probably. I did a little bit of experimenting as a teenager, but let's just say that I have plenty of eye candy with the local Ranger population constantly visiting the shop."

My guts clenched at the mention that implied multiple visits. "Who?"

Floss laughed, the sound tinkling like a thousand bells to my ears. Blood rushed south again, leaving me heady. "You can't be jealous of that. My boss is married to a Ranger, and Jake appears to be attached to Andy at the hip. Are you gonna break up that bromance?" she teased.

She hadn't answered my question, but I kept that to myself. Floss had already called me out over jealousy, and this—all of it—was meant to be fake. Except it wasn't. Nothing about this moment felt anything but true at all.

The waiter returned to take our orders, and we agreed on several tapas platters to pick at as we talked.

"It might be a mark against my record but hell, girl. I think I'd do just about anything for you." The words slipped free, and I knew without thinking about them that they were true. There was a certain symmetry to that thought that aligned with my previous one. I reached out to snag a wayward curl, wrapping her golden strands around the tip of my finger.

"I thought—" she started and broke off, her eyes wide, lush pink lips parted.

I cursed myself for not taking a deeper taste of her when I kissed her before but that had meant to be chaste, not the blood thrumming sort tonight had devolved into. Or evolved. I had no idea where this sort of crazy was headed, but hell did I want to be along for the ride with her.

"Stop thinking, Floss. Stop stressing or worrying or…anything. Just go with it." I'm sure I grinned like a loon, Dierks Bentley's '5-1-5-0' lyrics echoing in my head.

"Says the anxiety-ridden Ranger across the table." She recaptured the curl, winding it off my finger. "You scare me." But her answering smile belied the weight of her words.

"I scare myself most of the time. And probably half the people in the office, from what Andy said earlier."

Her brow dipped as she freed her hair, though she didn't move when I cupped my hand to her cheek instead, brushing the pad of my thumb across her velvet skin. "What did Andy say?"

"I try too hard and to just…"

"Let it go?" Her lips pursed, though her shoulders shook lightly.

I grinned ruefully. "Would you like me to sing it?"

"I mean, if you can sing?"

"Not in the slightest." I broke the contact with her, thumping my chest as I pretended to launch into song with no actual intention, watching for the telltale disappointment that swept across her gaze.

Floss raised her own fingers as though to press them to her cheek, then dropped her hand. "No, please don't sing." Her eyes widened, her cheeks matching the pink of her lips.

I dropped the act, leaning back with my wine glass in hand, still watching her, learning her. "You're pretty when you beg," I said in a low voice designed to keep her on edge.

Floss grabbed her wine glass, using it as a shield as she took a long drink. She put it back down and clasped her hands together over the white tablecloth, her fingers pink and tense where they intertwined.

I hid a smile; I wasn't the only one who was out of practice with this whole dating thing, fake or otherwise.

A plate arrived in front of me, filled with tiny, bite-sized pieces. Another arrived, then another. There was plenty to fill us up, or to graze while we talked and I teased her. I shifted in my seat, my jeans uncomfortably tight. Or maybe I was teasing us both. I'd run with this crazy vibe she responded to, but I wasn't rushing it. Not...yet.

Eating gave her a chance to stay silent, and slowly the flush receded from her cheeks. I couldn't wait for it to return.

Floss bit into an ocean trout *croqueta*, eying me. I'd had my fun; now it was her turn to dish it back at me. "Why did you become a cop?"

I raised an eyebrow, interested in the direction she took. "Not a Ranger?"

She shook her head with a slight smile and finished the crumbled morsel. "Nope. I wanna know what eighteen-year-old Acton Cunningham had in mind when he opted to join the police force." She leaned forward, placing her elbows on the table and lacing her hands under her chin.

"Fair enough. But you started me with an easy one. Hero worship."

Both eyebrows raised. "Who?"

"Think about it." I canceled a piece of beef tataki topped with shaved onion. "You know."

It didn't take her long to work it through. "Andy."

I nodded slowly. "He was two years above me at school. The jock kid with the golden smile who no one ever said anything negative about. He was always the first person to offer a hand, and ended up valedictorian for his year. When he announced he was going into law enforcement, it was an easy decision to follow. Just so happened it turned out to be something I was good at, too."

"Wow. I'm impressed."

"That a kid could have an idol through high school? I think most kids have one of those—just depends if it's someone close to home or not."

"But you followed through, all the way, and now…"

I shrugged, uncomfortable with her lightly veiled praise. "And now I'm ratcheting up my career level. Still following the hero's path."

"And you love it." She grabbed my fingers and squeezed gently. "I'm glad you found what you want to do with your life, Acton. It's not an easy thing."

My gaze narrowed. "Because you feel you haven't yet," I murmured.

Her hand dropped away. "No."

"Why'd you move from California?"

Floss pressed her lips together, then threw up her hands, jostling a dish. "Fuck it. I had no direction. I didn't actually have a place to live, not of my own, for years before Ella called and asked for help once she fell pregnant. I couch surfed for years, working small, easy pay jobs and spent my free hours on the sand. So I decided the responsible thing to do was to come here and get an actual rental," she grimaced, "which Andy helped me secure, and Ella gave me a job."

"And you love it." I threw her words back at her lightly, laughing when her eyes narrowed. "You're too cute. Seriously, though. Do you love it?"

"I— yes. Mostly." She bit her lip. "Wait, that sounds ridiculously ungrateful. I love working with plants. I just…wish that more of them were the growing sort."

"Getting your hands dirty, huh? Why don't you work a side hustle and become one of her suppliers, too?"

"Uh, can I do that in a rental property? Maybe if I could make a small greenhouse…" Her mind whirred—I could see it in the way her eyes brightened, how she sat up straighter. "Sorry, I geeked out there about green thumbs for a minute."

"Whatever works for you, Floss. There's no 'one size fits all' life or career path. It's whatever gives you the most joy, that wakes you up each morning with enough passion to keep going day after day."

"Wise words." Floss nodded.

We ate in silence after that for a period and when the dishes were empty, I rose and held out my hand. "Walk you home?"

She placed her fingers in mine, her head tilted back. "How do you know where I live?"

"Habit of a detective. Seriously, Ella messaged me your everything."

"I need to have words with that girl," Floss grumbled.

"Go easy on her. She's fairly testy when she's pregnant."

"Gorgeous, though." Floss let me pull her up. "Have you been on the other end of her temper?"

"No, but I've seen her rile up to Andy." I led her down to the street level, thanking the staff profusely as we passed. They'd done a fine job, and I'd paid them for the evening in advance which left us free to wander the few blocks to Floss' home.

We reached the end of the commercial area, where the soft glow from houses began to replace hard fluorescents. Her hand was still inside mine, and she hadn't pulled away.

"Thank you for tonight, for letting me learn more about you," she murmured as we reached the corner of the next block. "I— I haven't really done this before."

"Ever?" I hiked my eyebrows, turning to face her. "No one's taken you out?"

She shook her head. "No. I sort of met people through friends and I just…merged social groups, I guess. Everything was informal–beach life, student life, and I guess I went with it."

I recalled my own words to her from earlier in the evening. "This might be a little…different." *Overwhelming* was the word that came to mind but I kept that to myself. "Tell me anytime you need to back out, Floss. I won't hold you to a promise made under duress."

"It wasn't." She smiled, flicking her hair back off her shoulders. It glimmered gold in the streetlights as she pointed to a house a few down from where we stood. "I'm that one." Her voice trembled slightly.

She took a hesitant step forward, her hand firmly wrapped around mine. I narrowed my gaze, letting her tow me along. Suddenly, the comment about not being used to dating earlier took on new meaning. *A one-time, fun-time girl, huh?* She had to be. And no judgment from me—I might have earned a white Ranger's hat but I sure as hell was no saint.

But just because something was good didn't mean we had to rush it.

Curls draped over her face as she dug about one-handed into her purse when we reached the arched doorway of her house. Slowly and deliberately, so I wouldn't startle her, I caught her wrist in a firm grip and broke her focus. She stilled at the touch, her head rising to stare at me with wide eyes that were almost as tempting as those pillowy soft lips.

"Thanks for giving me a chance." I stared down at her, my own heart hammering. Her lips parted and my jeans tightened. *Not tonight.* Another night, perhaps; a plan began to form in my mind.

But not tonight.

"Do you want to come inside?" she asked my chest. Pink stained her cheeks as I found the side light and flicked it on, removing the shadows around us.

"Not tonight, Flossy." Her chin dipped a bit, and I crooked a knuckle to bring her eyes back level with mine. "I know I didn't ask you last time, but can I kiss you?" The words rang true because they were, but they were also designed to take the sting out of the rejection.

Because it wasn't really one—just postponing what I hoped we could be for the short period I'd have her in my life.

A smile took the fear out of her eyes as she nodded her consent, and in that moment, I wanted to know she'd be mine forever.

But she's not yours.

Because none of it was real.

Dipping my head, I pressed my mouth over hers, drawing in the sweet, floral scent of her that mingled with the honey taste of her desert and wanted to groan out loud. *She tastes like heaven.* I regretted that choice not to take her up on her invitation to go inside as she slid her hands around my shoulders, linking them behind my neck and rising onto her toes as high as she could to press against me.

Her lips parted when I traced my tongue along that soft pink pillow I'd been eyeing off all night, swallowing her sigh as I deepened the kiss. I tugged on her hair until she angled her head back, and she arched into me, her body fitting in the curve of mine to perfection.

"Are you sure you don't want to come inside?" she mumbled against my mouth when I let her up for air, still kissing me between words.

"Not as convinced as I was a moment ago, but no. I'll do one thing right, Flossy. But…" I rested my forehead to hers as I caught her shoulders and backed her against her door, snagging quick, open mouthed kisses. Her tongue tangled with mine, sending sensation prickling across the tops of my thighs and along my cock.

Ruching the material of her skirt in my fist at her waist, I pressed my knee between her thighs and up, relishing the little musical sigh that softened her body against mine.

"I thought Rangers were supposed to be gentlemen," she whispered, her eyes wide as I braced my forearms either side of her head, boxing her in.

She shivered in the space I created, arching to press her mouth against mine. I gave into the urge, kissing her harder, nipping and sucking on her bottom lip until I knew it would be rose red and swollen when I was done. The heat between our bodies rose as I pulsed my knee up against her pussy, her body already trying to ride out the impending orgasm as she rose onto her tiptoes to avoid the pressure that built when my knee rubbed against her through the thin material of her dress.

Her breath caught as she bore down, rubbing herself shamelessly against my jeans. I caught her hip in a firm grip when she came to herself and tried to pull away, refusing to let her ruin the pleasure, making her ride it out.

"Acton," she whimpered, her head falling forward to rest her cheek against my chest, clinging to me with both arms wrapped around my back.

She trembled there as I scooped her into my arms, tucking her curves to my chest.

"God, you feel good there." *Right*. Like I shouldn't walk away from her. But if I went inside her house, I knew I'd end up worshiping her body on my knees, with little doubt of how the night would end.

Not. Yet.

Tension tightened in my chest until I growled softly into her hair, inhaling her flowers and honey scent, heady with the taste of her still on my tongue.

"What happened to the gentleman?" she murmured, her face still buried over my heart.

"I'm just a man, Floss. Not a saint." I kissed her hair and held her for a little while longer, memorizing every inch of her, how she felt pressed to me, the space she took up in my arms.

When I kissed her goodnight and watched her walk inside her house and lock me out, I could still feel the imprint of her lips pressed over my heart. I'd been too scared to risk falling in love again. But as I walked home, night air sliding cold fingers inside my shirt, my hands pressed into my pockets, I wondered if I might have made the wrong choice in not tying for something real with Floss.

My heart ached at the mere memory of her; soft lips, blue eyes flashing with mischief. The cute as a button smile a man could lay down his heart for, even when he was hell-bent on keeping himself apart from any such risk.

I wondered if I might not have a choice.

CHAPTER FOUR

FLOSS

Three days after my date with Acton, I stood at the base of a podium wearing a borrowed dress that fit me like a sheath, a broad brim hat over my eyes in the unseasonal blistering heat, clapping politely. A Ranger flanked me on either side and though I had more confidence than I could usually spend on a daily basis, I felt small between them.

Acton and Andy's combined presence could be overwhelming, and it wasn't just due to their size and broad shoulders. When they stood together, both dressed in pressed button down shirts, white hats and boots, they could be brothers. Something about the way they stood offered an innate measure of protection, and while Acton might say he followed Andy into the police force and then to the Rangers unit, he more than held his own. For all his concern about not fitting in, his stance and easy camaraderie with his unit made it clear he fit in. It was just up to him to accept that it happened, and he just hadn't noticed yet.

On the stage, Acton's boss, Rhys Archer, presented awards for a local citizen's charity, and by the time he reached the end of the first round, my hands were already sore from constantly applauding. The man himself was intimidating as could be, his shirt sweat and stain free under the midday sun, looking as though he'd just stepped out of an icebox. Red hair glinted beneath his white hat that matched Acton and Andy's.

Andy discreetly pulled his phone from his pocket as it buzzed, and grimaced. "Gotta go. Make my excuses," he muttered over my head.

"Baby?" Acton asked out of the corner of his mouth.

"I can go, if you're needed here?" I offered.

Archer threw a heavy-browed look over his shoulder in our direction. We fell silent.

"It's fine. I got it," Andy answered belatedly, already falling out of line.

The man behind him stepped up to fill his place. "Take your time, old man," the blond Ranger called, grinning and offering a quick wave when their boss turned and glared at him in full.

"How are you not dead after that stare?" I whispered to Jake's general amusement.

"He's got a bit of that sort of air about him, doesn't he?" he murmured in my ear, bending low to speak over the applause. He jostled, and someone's elbow hit my spine.

"Ow," I whispered, unable to keep my pained gasp at bay.

This time, Archer glared at both of the men on either side of me and raised a querying brow in my direction.

I gave him a small smile, mortified to be under his inspection, and only breathed normally once he turned away. "Jesus," I muttered. "I'm not cut out for this, Acton."

"You're doing great." His hand brushed my lower back in an intimate gesture of support. "And you look beautiful."

"Thanks." I tugged the sides of the powder blue dress that came with a matching twin set. "I feel like a matron."

"You look far from it," Jake offered on my other side with a wink.

Acton growled something under his breath as the next round of applause broke out that I couldn't quite hear. Jake tilted his head, looking between us and his smile disappeared. He studied me as I stood unmoving between the men. I wiggled my feet, trying not to fidget under his stare, and wished Andy hadn't had to go. The ceremony thankfully finished a few minutes later and I ducked out from Jake's watchful presence, catching Acton's hand to lead him to a group of women who crowed and clucked around every Ranger they could find.

"Andy, this is Regina. She and her ladies entertain the children's ward each week. She does clown make up, and Elaine creates cute balloon animals."

"The kids must adore you," Acton said to both women, who flushed and chattered on until another woman drew them away for a press photo. Acton took the opportunity to slip away.

I followed him to an iced tea stand, grateful for the cool, sweet liquid, eyeing off a pair of local cops who tried to catch the eye of a pair of young ladies who only had eyes for the white hats in the congregation.

"Those poor uniforms don't stand a chance," I murmured, pressing the plastic cup to my cheeks, though the ice had already melted. "I thought you were all for photos and the like? I didn't get dressed up for no reason," I joked, elbowing him a little in the ribs.

"Today isn't about me and my career," Acton muttered, staring over my head.

I frowned, turning to follow his line of sight. Jake returned Acton's stare and raised a takeaway coffee mug. "Then, what am I doing here?" I smiled, but Acton didn't notice. His hand remained on the small of my back, what had been a reassuring presence became a tense moment.

"Be right back," Acton said. He gave my waist a quick squeeze and disappeared into the crowd—no mean feat when he stood a head and a half above the rest of the people in it on a usual day, but today the audience was full of men who looked just like him.

I clutched my empty iced tea cup until the plastic creaked. Looking around, I found a table and placed it at the back corner, thanking the white-haired lady who peered at me shortsightedly.

It had been a mistake. Without something to hold, or Andy or Acton to talk to, I found myself too alone in a large group of people who I had nothing in common with whatsoever, except for the man who just left me on my own.

Didn't he say he wouldn't do that?

I tried to recall if that had been part of our initial bartering over my side of the fake relationship proposition. Maybe I'd made it up, or thought that was part of his promise to me.

Either way, I desperately wanted an exit strategy, though none was forthcoming.

"He's off with Archer." A tall shadow, though not as long as the one Acton cast, covered me.

I blinked at the white-haired Ranger. "Do you guys come short at all?"

Jake shrugged. "An old hang-up from the six foot two inches police standard, I suppose, if an outdated one. Sure, a tall man looks good in a shirt but height has nothing to do with his brain capacity."

"True," I allowed, squeezing my hands together. "Ah, did you say Acton was with his—your boss?" I stumbled over the words, peering around him at the empty stage. Neither Acton nor his boss were anywhere in sight.

"How are you managing?" Jake asked casually.

I looked up at the forced light tone. "Did you just try to bullshit me?"

Someone nearby coughed. I ignored it.

Jake's grin widened. "Acton Man has bitten off more than he can handle with this little spitfire, hasn't he?"

"He's fine. I just don't—" I pressed my lips into a tight line, used to being able to speak my mind and missing the freedom of it. "Can you point me in his direction, please?"

Jake sent me a pitying look I wasn't certain I'd earned. "Hon, if you're not comfortable with whatever Cunningham goaded you into, you're not stuck to it. I'll walk you home or to your car if you need."

I blinked at him. "I beg your pardon?" My skin prickled beneath his steady stare, leaving me in a hyper aware state. Conversation around me grew to a roar and I couldn't focus. "What do you mean?"

"You're not dumb, because you're Ella's friend and she's a smart girl and likes clever company. So don't behave that way. We both know you're not really dating Cunningham."

"That doesn't leave you free to hit on me," I snapped, then winced.

"Damn," Jake murmured, grinning like a lunatic. "My girl would have my balls tied to a spit roast if I cheated on her and there's no chance in hell of that. You're cute, but she's mine."

"Good to know." I circled him warily. "What's your point, Ranger?"

"Oh, hell. He's going to have a time with you. He's over there." Jake spun me on my heel and pointed in the direction of the far side of the crowd. "If you need him to have a wake up call, tell me and I'll take pleasure in bitch slapping him for whatever he's not doing right."

"He's doing just fine," I said defensively, folding my arms over my chest, though Ella had warned me not to. The dress rose and hot air flicked the backs of my thighs.

"Uh huh. Don't get attached to the man. That's all I'm going to say. Save yourself a broken heart, huh?" Jake gave me a gentle push between the shoulder blades, propelling me into the crowd.

When I looked back, he was gone and I stood alone in the middle of the crowd.

Again.

"It was a long day, huh?" Acton draped his hand around my waist, his gaze fluttering across the crowd while my heart clenched.

It was one date. One kiss. That's all. As a thank you in advance.

Well, it was two kisses, technically, but who's counting? The man just wanted company over events to look like the empty-hearted politician he obviously was because my own heart clenched every time I looked at him. I knew going into this it would be a bad idea, but Ella and Andy convinced me of Acton's honest, good nature.

So why did I feel like a wallflower left out to dry in the late afternoon sun?

The thought that the event was over had been false in every sense—at least as fake as the pretend cuddles Acton put on in public. Around us, people talked and networked while I stood stiffly by Acton's side, collecting pitying looks from a parade of Rangers who passed by to congratulate him on his position in the unit. A handful of cops spoke to us too, though they didn't seem to see the undercurrents between us the way Acton's colleagues did.

I'd rather be anywhere but here.

An elderly couple waved their goodbyes, others starting to leave the ceremony site. I could barely remember what it was all for and this was just my first event with Acton. Every time I looked at him, my body rebelled, aching for his attention. It couldn't happen; it wasn't what he wanted, which was the main reason I'd wanted to invite him in after our date. If I could just get the gorgeous Ranger out of my system, and start getting over him, I wouldn't be feeling like this now.

But no…Acton had to be a gentleman and a sinner all at once, declining my invitation but giving me an orgasm at the door.

Wham, bam, goodnight ma'am.

And I stood beside him now, looking for all the world like a lovelorn teen…which wasn't far off from the real thing. I'd started to fall for the knight-in-shining-armor —or in this case, a white hat—that Acton presented. He kissed like a bee to honey, and he'd read exactly what my body needed before I did after a night talking and eating together. Plus there were those damn shoulders that made him so much sexier than any other man at the event, while I stood there looking like hired help. Worse than that, I stood there as a paid escort.

I'd hooked myself out.

No wonder the man didn't bother to look at me.

I coughed softly into my fist, breaking back against the flood of pity tears that speared across my eyes and willed them back by determination alone. "If you're wrapping it up here, I might walk home."

I might have considered an endearment or a jibe after the end of the comment once, but not after today. I'd known acton cunningham for less than a week and he had my head spinning off my shoulders already.

"Mmmhm?" Acton looked down at me as though surprised I was still there. His fingers flexed on my shoulder, realization crossing his features. I sighed and, just as I thought he might apologize for his distracted nature, he nodded and slipped his hand free of my skin. "Thanks so much for helping me out today, Floss. It's been a long time on your feet."

"It's not that bad," I lied. I had blisters blooming on my heels the size of pancakes.

"Well, then. Appreciate it." He doffed his hat— *really?*—and eaved over my head, gone before I could think through what just happened, or more to the point—what *didn't* happen.

Swallowing back the wash of tears, I headed back across the field of vacating party-goers, all chattering and a few stumbling from excess punch, but I barely saw anyone. My delivery driver bumped into me, still muttering about her parcels and gave me a wave, sweat beading across her face. Her hair stood out frizzier than ever as I held myself together long enough to find the nearest taxi rank, sliding into the first available without checking if anyone had called it. Only when the door closed, locking me into the shadowy, stuffy interior, did I kick off the too-tall heels that didn't quite fit me right and let the tears fall.

.

CHAPTER FIVE

ACTON

I stared at my stationary ceiling fan and tried not to think about how big and empty my bed had become. Sleep never came easy for me, not after an incident or arrest at work, or while I was working through a case. Certainly not when instead of tracking the routes the drugs made through the city in my head, all I could see when I closed my eyes was a pair of sparkling blue eyes and beachy blonde hair tangled in messy waves and how soft her lips were when I kissed her.

That never should have happened.

The idea of pretending she was my girlfriend to the general populace was to form a solid baseline for myself. Stability, honest and steadfast. Once, those things might have described me, but after seeing Floss shoved into a dress and heels that clearly weren't hers, her sexy bedhead turned into a glossy french roll and her blue eyes dulled to the hazy blue of the sky instead of glittering like an ocean in summer, I knew I'd got it wrong.

That, and the fact was that a few of the event's participants ended up in the emergency room. Three were home now, and had no idea how the drugs had gotten into their system, and none were habitual users at all.

One elderly man hadn't woken up yet.

My stomach clenched over itself. Andy had enough to deal with while Ella struggled through the end of her pregnancy—the third trimester, I thought, though I knew next to nothing about babies other than how to make one.

I wish I'd taken Floss up on her invite at the end of our date.

I'd broken her, ruined her natural sparkle that drew me to her, from the crazy named plant to her cheeky banter on our date.

How soft and sweet and so damn sexy she felt in my arms when I kissed her goodnight, like it was the beginning of something special.

No, the only way to make her happy would be to call it off. I tossed my phone in the air and tried not to let it hit me in the face when the thing buzzed in my hand. I checked my watch. Past midnight. I hadn't gotten the impression she was a night owl, but hell, I'd been wrong before.

Floss: *How's your investigation going?*

She'd reached out in the middle of the night, which meant I'd screwed up with her worse than I thought. I wanted to talk about work, about the investigation, but that was something I'd do with a real partner and Floss…I cursed and rocked my head back on my pillow, option to reply with something inane. Maybe that was a mistake, too.

Acton: *Can't sleep either, huh?*

Floss: *I was thinking about the event. You were…distracted.*

Acton: *Yeah, I suck as a date. It's official. I'd say it's why I don't do this shit but I'd be lying.*

Floss: *What's the real reason?*

Acton: *I'm a coward. My heart still remembers what broken feels like*

Floss: *Aren't you the romantic?*

She followed that comment up with a tiny pair of pink hearts.

Acton: *Better believe it. Sometimes what I feel just doesn't make it to the surface.*

Floss: *Ohh, denial. Burn, baby.*

I snorted.

Acton: *Appreciate it. Thanks.*

Floss: *Well. Sorry I woke you up or whatever. Night.*

I stared at the message, but there were no dots under it that said she was still thinking. The conversation was over. I'd killed it, and I had no idea how.

Acton: *Goodnight, Floss. I'll talk to you tomorrow.*

I had to let her go. She was needy one minute, and throwing up walls the next. I had no idea how to break them down, only how to make sure I didn't screw her life up any further by trying to make her something she wasn't. The funny thing was, I didn't need to, after everything. Ansy had talked up the relationship thing early on, but Archer me aside halfway through the reception. I could still hear his words inside my head.

"If you bring a woman to an event, it's courtesy to stay with her." Archer stood with his hands clasped behind his back as we watched our third OD carted away in an ambulance.

I'd said goodbye to Floss over an hour prior, and I winced when the realization hit me that I hadn't checked up that she got home. I withdrew my phone from my pocket, turning it over in my hand. "You're right. I'm sorry."

"I'm not the pretty girl dating you, Cunningham, and she won't be either if you don't get your act together." Rhys Archer turned blazing eyes on me that stripped away every inch of the bullshit I'd put up as a facade.

"Noted, sir."

"Don't 'sir' me, not after you've helped me clean up a woman who almost drowned in a puddle of her own vomit." He sluiced a hand through sweat-streaked hair and put his hat back on. "You're a solid Ranger, Cunningham. That's not in doubt. But right now your personal integrity is."

"Ouch." I winced and nodded sharply. "I'll work on it."

"I remember having this conversation with another young Ranger not more than a year ago. Jake pulled his head out of his ass, and because of that, he's still on my team. Choice is up to you." Archer gave me a nod and turned on his heel, speaking softly to the paramedics who cleaned up the scene around us.

I flicked the screen of my phone up, ready to send out an apology to Floss. Somewhere in the background, screams and shouts started. Sighing, I slipped my phone back into my pocket, turning on my heel and taking off at a job.

Being a cop had been so much easier than this political bullshittery.

I blinked at the ceiling and checked my phone again. Floss hadn't sent anything else, and I still hadn't sent the apology message, what with all the distractions and interviewing family friends and victims at the hospital. I threw my phone once more, letting it freefall to the pillow beside me, and wondered why I'd bothered to buy a larger bed that suited more than one person when I was the only person who slept in it, and my legs still hung off the end of the bed.

I have to let her go.

She should be here, playing some mischief or letting me roll her onto her back and discover everything her body wanted. But I was too selfish to break it off with Floss without saying sorry in my own way first. My hand was on my cock as I thought about what I could do to make it up to her in a way she'd understand best.

I finished setting up what I needed for Floss an hour before she was due to arrive at the rustic ranch I'd borrowed from Bear Winslow for the night. The man was out on some overnight trek, the sort the mountain man favored that took him well away from the rest of civilization.

Candles created a curved path to a small hillock where I'd erected an arbor out of leftover timber from Bear's shed. He'd given me carte blanche to do whatever I needed—I took that to mean within reason— for my night with her, the one she'd grudgingly accepted my invitation for, according to Andy. Not only had I broken her, now she was gunshy.

Another thing I needed to make up for.

Hence my change of Bear's landscape. The big Ranger wasn't the materialistic sort, and he spent less time at the ranch he'd built from scratch than he did out in a space he'd literally etched for himself between a canyon and a rock face at the far end of his enormous property. The place was far enough from the city lights to give a starscape like nothing else, but close enough that Floss wouldn't have to get off the blacktop until she turned onto his drive.

I left a wreath of orchids at the fence line for Floss to find. Step one. Dinner under the stars was the second part of my plan. I hoped she'd let me get to stage three. Checking my work was complete, I worked my way back to the house to change and shower before she turned up and caught me in the buff.

A stupid ass smile spread over my face as I checked the wine was in the fridge at that idea, thoughts of Floss filling my head as I doused myself in cold water and soap suds. By the time I was finished, her car had turned onto the long drive that wound its way before a plume of red dust that kicked up behind her vehicle.

Floss was early.

Good thing she wasn't the only organized one. I grinned as I buttoned my shirt. I didn't care if she kicked my ass for how I treated her at the awards ceremony. All I wanted was a chance to put that sparkle back in her eyes.

Feeling her body pressed to mine would be a bonus—if she let me.

I headed out to meet her at the cleared yard where I parked my own truck. Her small yellow bubble looked cutely out of place next to my red giant. "Glad you made it out here easy enough."

I grabbed for the driver's door as she rose, her blue gaze flashing over mine, half panicked and half defiant. I loved one and could lose the other, knowing I'd keep that defiant streak in her if I got any choice in the matter at all.

It wasn't like she'd let that happen, and that was another thing I loved about her.

She dressed in a pink and red flowy dress that swung around her knees, looking sexy and stunning as hell. Tan wedge sandals tied around her ankles with a dozen straps knotted on either side of her shins. She tossed back that glorious hair, her eyes sparkling blue under the sunset streaked sky.

Floss nodded behind me. "You put on a good show, Cunningham."

I raised both brows. "I do, huh?"

"Your house?" She gestured to the ranch house.
I shook my head. "Hell, no. This belongs to another Ranger who let me borrow it for the evening." I held out a hand and stopped breathing.

"Doesn't he need it?" She looked at me curiously, then took my hand, stepping toward the house.

"This way." I led her around the side of the building to the row of candles that flickered beneath the darkening sky.

"Bear is a…particular sort of crazy. He doesn't like people, and he doesn't like talking. More of a solo flier. He does a lot of undercover cattle poaching rings and the like. Offered this up because he'd come into town and I didn't want to refuse the offer."

"It's beautiful." Fliss closed her mouth but sent me a sideways glance, her brow doing, as if to ask *what's this about*? Though the words didn't make it past her lips.

I stopped as she took in everything around her. The setting sun that sank below the far mountain range, the wide open vista across the plains. The candle light pathway that led to the top of the hillock I spent the day building.

"It is. Like you." I turned her to face and blew out a sharp breath. "I've owed you an apology since I walked into your shop and broke your orchids."

"Is that why there was one of the ga—"

I held up a hand. "Wait. I memorized this and I'm shit at speeches, so let me ramble for a bit." Floss closed her mouth and sent me a bemused glance. I waited until I was sure she wouldn't talk and then started again. "I took you out for dinner, and I didn't go inside with you after. I should have." I went off the script and probably the reservation with that one, reaching out to toy with one of her curls. "And the next time I saw you I was so preoccupied with what was going on around me, I couldn't see you. And you looked so pretty, all done up, but it wasn't you. I'd stuffed you into the role of someone else's life, or wife, and none of those things were what I wanted for you. So this is my crazy ass way of saying sorry. If you'll let me."

Floss stared at me open-mouthed. She leaned forward, cupping a hand around her mouth, stage whisper style. "You weren't wrong about the speech delivery, but that was cute, Acton. I accept."

"The apology? Flossy, I haven't gotten started yet."

She crinkled her nose. "Flossy?"

"Yup. You're mine tonight. Or I can feed you and make sure you get home safe."

Say you'll stay with me.

"You want me here with you, all night?" she clarified carefully. Her head tilted to one side as she considered me. I nodded, not trusting my voice. Finally, she stepped forward, pressing her hands to my chest. "Then yes. I'll stay."

I didn't answer her because I was already too busy working my hands through her silky curls and kissing the hell out of her.

CHAPTER SIX

FLOSS

Acton Cunningham was a conundrum. One minute he was the distant Texas Ranger intent on fulfilling his duty, the next he was pulling crazy romantic dates out of his perfectly carved tush and dragging me along with his wild dreams.

And here Andy and Ella thought I'd be the wild one.

I took the arm he offered, his skin warm beneath the long sleeves, as though he'd just gotten out of the shower. I'd clung to my sinking emotions over the last few days until Acton called and said he wanted me to go on another date with him.

My first reaction had been a big '*hell, no*' but the man begged, and if I were honest with myself, my heart melted the moment I saw him again. Not that his efforts and easy grin made what happened at the last event alright, but it did dim the anxiety that had been occupying my chest since I saw him last.

"You didn't have to go to all this trouble, you know." I mean, he did, but I wasn't about to admit that I liked what he'd done.

"'Course I did. Romantic at heart and all." The corner of his mouth quirked up, belaying the shadows that crept into the corners of his gaze. He gave my arm a squeeze, and all I saw was the genuine man who had been too scared to ask me—or any girl—on a real date, so he asked me on a fake one.

"You're doing fine," I reassured him, though he didn't seem to need it.

Maybe it was me who was nervous—that would be a first. But everything about this man set my emotions into a hyper aware state. Even the cool night air that brushed over my arms and wound its way around the open back of my dress left me shivery and hot all at once.

The candles glimmered at our ankles as he led me along the pathway to an arbor that looked covered in yellow cloth, but as we came closer, I realized he'd made a bower covered—every single inch of the structure—in flowers. Beneath it lay a picnic blanket with extra rugs piled at each corner. Pillows filled in the edges of the gassed space and a tray of food and chilled wine was set in the middle.

"Acton," I breathed. "Where did you get all these?"

He gave me a small smile, looking down at me with a hooded gaze. "Ella helped," he murmured softly. "I mean it,

Floss. You deserve so much more than a man ignoring you when you were doing me a favor. I let work get in the way."

"It was all about your work," I protested, though my mind screamed, *take the compliment!* inside my head. But I had been there to support him, and I'd let my fear of being abandoned fill my head with the wrong sort of thoughts. "I should have been by your side the entire time."

"It's okay, Flossy. I get it." He grazed his fingers across my cheek, catching my hair and drawing me closer. "Forgive me?"

"I— Of course," I mumbled, flustered. Heat rose in my cheeks at the way he looked at me, hungry, like a starved man. I wasn't used to anyone looking at me like that, or being the center of anyone's attention, and kind of hated it and loved it too. I sucked in a breath and detached myself from him. "How long did it take you to do this?"

I spied one of the handheld spritz bottles Ella had stashed around her shop to keep everything looking bright and healthy.

"All day," he admitted, rubbing a hand over the back of his neck. "I didn't start the flowers until the sun was setting, as I didn't want them to wilt in the heat. Took me a while to build the gazebo though."

He'd built the entire thing. I blinked at him. "You have a very nice friend," I murmured. Not many people would let you come into their home or land and construct something random for a date—even a fake one.

Yet again the sense hit me that this wasn't fake at all and that I was finally getting to see the real Acton Cunningham.

"I'd rather think about you than him right now." Acton wound an arm around my waist, drawing me back into his body as I studied the flowers.

I traced over one bright yellow petal that turned into a deep pinkish crimson in the candlelight and gave the bloom a squeeze. Its little mouth popped open and snapped back when I released them. "Snapdragons. You remembered." That blasted form he sent through asking me all my vitals and my favorite flowers when we first met. It had been an unemotional, unattached approach, cold and sterile. This…this was anything but cold or lifeless. I smiled at him over my shoulder as he dipped his head, his lips gazing at the corners of my mouth. My body tensed, a frisson of goosebumps rising over my skin.

"I asked you for a reason, Floss." He swept my hair over my shoulder and kissed the back of my neck, working his way to the curve of my throat, sucking lightly on the spot there. I shivered again, clinging to his arm that held me up.

"But that was before—" I started.

Acton caught my jaw in his fingertips, tipped my head back and kissed me.

If I thought he'd kissed me after our first date, I had been totally and utterly wrong. Acton swept his tongue along my bottom lip until I opened to him, then he delved inside, cupping the back of my head to angle me the way he wanted. A soft whimper drew from my throat as I reached one arm back to wrap around his neck, telling myself it was for balance when all I wanted was to be as close to him as possible.

His fingers massaged the back of my neck in sweeping circles, sending that same thrill over my body but deeper this time, awakening nerves and driving arousal far more than only surface-level. He kissed me harder until I arched for him, letting him mold me to his tall frame as he wanted, always supporting me with the arm that held me in a steady grip, gathering my dress up against my side one inch at a time.

"How hungry are you right now?" he rasped as he broke the contact long enough to press kisses along my cheek and down my neck.

I rested my head against his shoulder, ruffling his hair with my fingers as I stared up at the diamond studded midnight velvet sky above us. "Don't stop."

"Don't stop?"

"Please, Acton." I tugged on his hair and was rewarded with his lips pressed to mine as he swung me into his arms and walked us over to a pasha-like pile of wide pillows.

I sank into the nest he created as he passed me a glass of bubbling champagne. His gaze darkened impossibly as he passed me the cold crystal. "Drink?"

"Didn't I say not to stop?" I grumbled, taking a small sip, then another. Liquid honeysuckle trickled down my throat and I sighed, then it hit me. "This is Moët." I didn't have to question that; the soft bubbles that burst in my mouth were my favorite, and I'd had it on a few rare special occasions in my life.

"It is." He sipped from his glass and carefully put it down on a small stand. I passed him mine and he shelved that one too. "Floss—" His voice strained, roughening at the edges as he caught my hand and knelt at my side.

He never got further in whatever speech he had planned because I was too impatient. Rising on my elbows, I tipped my head back and arced up as he leaned down. Our mouths met in a crash of kisses and wild emotions. Hands caught as we tugged at each other's clothes in a flurry of need until skin pressed to skin and he eased his way between my legs.

If I thought Acton looked good in a shirt, he was a god without it. Wide shoulders were framed with just the right amount of muscle; hard, flat planes that spoke of strength and commitment without being overly bulky. I ran my fingers along his chest, scraping my nails lightly over his nipples.

He growled at the teasing contact, leaning down to rest his forehead against mine. "If we don't slow down, I won't be able to do all the things I planned with you tonight." He scraped rough knuckles along the insides of my thighs, widening the space between my legs so he could settle there, his erect cock rubbing against my entrance.

"Plans are overrated," I gasped as his cock slid against my clit. Painful spasms of pleasure wracked my body, and I hadn't even started. "Plus, I like being on top."

"If that's what you like," Acton murmured. He wound an arm around us, sliding down my body as he flipped us so I straddled his shoulders.

"That's not what I meant!" I yelped, though the sound softened as his lips and tongue teased my swollen pussy lips.

Sucking and nibbling, he tasted every inch of me, sliding his tongue back and forth from clit to crack. I shuddered as he thrust his tongue and two fingers deep inside me, clenching down on the invasion, my orgasm rising fast but just out of reach.

"That's it, come for me, Floss." He added a third finger and sucked my clit into his mouth hard.

Starlight burst behind my eyelids, obliterating everything around me but the feel of his warmth between my legs. The pressure built on as he played with my pussy, fingers crooked inside me to hit that sensitive spot that drew my orgasm out until it blended with a smaller one.

I sagged over his shoulders, pushing sweat-heavy curls back from my face with trembling hands. "That wasn't fair. You surprised me."

"You said plans were overrated," he reminded me, sliding my body the length of his, covering us both in my sweat until my legs fell open either side of his hips. "Still wanna be on top? I don't want to wear you out." He kissed me tenderly, framing my face with broad, calloused hands.

"I'll stay right here," I murmured. I tasted myself on his lips, and the unusual sensation made me tremble faster.

He fumbled to one side, coming up with a condom pack. The foil crinkled in his fingers as he placed it into my hand. "Would you?"

I nodded, tearing the pack open sliding back a little to clasp his rigid cock in my hand. Acton hissed his next breath, his thighs tensing beneath me. I worked my hand along the smooth skin, flicking my thumb over the mushroom head, back and forth until his head fell back and he groaned.

"Hell, Floss. I told you…" His cock pulsed in my hand, and I gave him mercy.

"So you did." I slipped the condom over him, discarding the packet, and straddled him. His hardness pressed against my heat. I rocked, sliding the arousal that slicked us both over him, then lowered myself in a steady drop until my thighs touched his.

I wanted to say something dirty, but I didn't have any breath left. Acton filled me to the brim, stretching me to a tight fullness I'd never felt before.

"*Christ*, Floss," he grated through clenched teeth. "You're so goddam tight." He caught my gaze and my hips and held me tight. "Bounce."

His words echo weirdly in my head, as though I was already floating high above him. My thighs work on instinct, rising me along the length of his cock to pause at his wide head, letting him stretch me before his hands on my hip pushed me back down. Whatever degree of control I thought I had was whisked away as Acton pushed me down again and again.

"Please," I gasped as he thrust up into me. White flashes edged my vision.

"You're close," he murmured, freeing up one hand to clasp mine. "Show me what you like."

I wanted to tell him I didn't have the brainpower or focus to do any such thing, but I didn't have the breath for that either. Acton was relentless, tearing into me as he linked our fingers, dragging the tips through my wetness and back to my clit.

"Touch yourself," he demanded, his gaze flicking from my face to our hands.

I nodded, moaning, and swept small circles over my clit, making our hands work together by some miracle of coordination. Tightness built low in my belly. I gripped his cock with my walls, rocking as the tendrils of pleasure unfurled inside me. Slow at first, my body tensed against the onslaught, then softening. My head tipped back and I cried my release to the sky.

Acton worked with me through my orgasm, and I looked down to see our hands still linked as my body softened.

I pulled my hand free, pressing both palms to his chest. "That was—" I gasped breath into a too small lung capacity. "I've never—"

"Fuck me, you're beautiful," Acton growled, pushing up to catch my face in his hand sand kissing me soundly. His cock thickened inside me and I moaned again. "Link your legs around me." I let him rearrange me into a pretzel that cuddled his hips, his hands landing on my ass and squeezing tight. "Lean on me. I've got you."

Acton thrust up into me, his hips flexing sharply as he pinned me against his cock. Once, then again, then— His hips pistoned into me as I dropped my forehead to his shoulder, clinging to him with my nails and licking the sweat lazily from his throat.

His body rocked mine until his thrusts jerked out of sequence. Heat rolled over me as he grew rougher, clutching my body tight to his. The feel of his cock swelling inside me combined with his roar threw me back into the land of bliss, and I collapsed with him into a world of pillows, beating hearts and safety.

CHAPTER SEVEN

ACTON

The sun hadn't hit the valley floor when I woke with Floss curled in my arms. My heart nearly tore at the sight of her sleeping heavily on me, like she trusted me to care for her. After the first round of incredible sex we picked at the fruit platter and wine, barely talking but always touching or kissing. I'd never been so comfortable with a woman with both of us naked for so long. Everywhere her lips touched me seared, like she'd marked me from the inside out as hers.

And all I wanted was to take her home, wrap her in my sheets and never leave.

But she'd shown me that my work got in the way of a relationship. The best I could do was give us both a better memory than the last we'd shared, and I was intent on making our hours last.

I shifted her body so she slipped off me onto the pillow pile, draping the blankets around her in a soft snuggly nest. I slid between her thighs, already hard at the sight of her. She mumbled sleepily as I kissed her lips, soft and pouty from last night. We'd been rough and now I wanted to give her a different sort of memory.

Her legs fell open as I covered my cock with a fresh condom, tracing the soft flesh of her inner thighs with my fingertips. She shivered in her sleep, rolling slightly, but I pressed my hands to her shoulders, flattening her beneath my body as I inched my way inside her hot and ready pussy.

She sighed, her eyelids fluttering open as I buried myself inside her.

"Morning, beautiful."

Her breath stalled against my mouth as she shifted beneath my weight, her body tightening at the shock of the intrusion. Her moaning my name was the first thing I heard from her as I rocked gently, getting her used to my size.

"Morning," she gasped, sliding her heels around the backs of my thighs to press into my ass. "Oh, god. Are you always going to wake me up like this?"

I stilled, bearing into her a little deeper. She frowned, but I moved again, sliding out and back into a rhythm her body showed me was the right one for her. Her hips jerked, and I held her to the blanket, kissing her while my heart pounded. I worked my thumb in a line along the inside of her hip as I thrust into her again, and she arched at the sensitive spot.

Her shattered cry as she came might have been the most beautiful thing I'd ever heard. The sun crested as she threw her head back, reveling in the pleasure that threaded its way through her body. She gripped my forearms, clinging to me through her orgasm as her bolster.

"So beautiful," I murmured, kissing her gently.

My control held tight in check, unlike the night before, I worked her body through a series of increasing waves as she clung to me, kissing her every time she came on my cock, praising her. She shivered, begging and whimpering until my own need rocked the foundation I'd built, my hips snapping harder and dragging me into my own euphoria as I exploded inside her.

Sunlight warmed my back where she traced patterns along my spine when I raised my head, licking and kissing my way up her neck. Floss giggled, batting at me with gentle hands, the tension worn out of both of us, and stared at me with eyes filled with—

Fuck, if this isn't a girl I could fall in love with.

Or maybe that already happened. From the way she looked at me, I was pretty sure she felt the same way. I kissed her again and held her until she wriggled.

"I hate to break this moment but I really need to use the bathroom."

"You got it." I brushed my lips across her temple, squeezing her gently.

She rose and dressed, running back along the path to the house. Bear had told me not to bother locking it. He didn't and he reasoned we'd be as safe as he was well away from the general populace. Lying back with my hands laced behind my head, I understood his reasoning.

Maybe getting out of the city wasn't a bad idea. I could keep my apartment, rent it maybe, and get something small, away from everything. For the first time in weeks since I'd joined Andy's unit my mind was clear. Out here there was no unnecessary chatter apart from the scant wildlife that made their own noises, though my peace was towed at least fifty percent to the woman bouncing along the path to me.

"If you're walking that well then I didn't do my job properly," I muttered against her mouth.

She laughed, slapping at me, as I worked my hands beneath her dress to free her panties from her legs. "You can't be serious."

"You're right. I'm not." I grinned though inside I had never felt more solemn.

I made love to my girl again as the world awoke, savoring every touch and kiss and moan, framing the moments for later. We packed up in silence and I kissed her again at her car, promising to drop in to see her at work later in the week. Tucking a yellow and pink flower behind her ear I watched as she drove away, my heart overfilled in my chest as though the damn thing would burst. I didn't think I'd care.

Then I packed up the mess I'd made of Bear's yard, cleaned the rooms I'd used in prep and his shed and headed back to work. By the time Bear's house was a speck in my rearview mirror, my head was back in my investigation, my stolen hours with Floss a memory packed tightly away and locked with care.

"You looked after that girl you're towing about yet?" Jake groused as I passed his coffee across his desk.

For a too-long minute I considered throwing the cup at him, but the flash in his eyes warned me on more than one front.

I nodded jerkily. "I'm sorting it."

"You'd better." The man who'd apparently decided to play big brother to Floss leaned back in his leather seat and crossed his ankles on his wooden desk.

It took everything in me not to scoff at him. Instead, I kept my face a mask and delivered coffees around the room, then headed to Andy's desk. "Anything new?"

"Other than us not figuring this thing out? Not a chance." He shook his head and drained half his coffee in one gulp.

"How long have you been here?"

Andy peered at me. "As in here, here? Is this a trick question?"

I took in his rumpled shirt and shitty shaving job. "You didn't get home last night."

"Is that optional?"

"Sleep usually isn't considered a choice." Guilt swamped me. "I'm sorry I've left you alone on this."

Andy waved a hand my way. "I'm sure I'll call in my fair share of favors when the baby is born."

"How's Ella doing?"

"Round, cute as all fuck, and hungry. I've never seen her eat so many spring rolls in my life."

I laughed. "Sounds like she's doing fine then."

"I'll take that." Andy eyed me. "How's Floss?"

"Best fucking night of my life." I spoke to his desk.

"But?"

"It can't work. I need to be here and I'm…. single-minded."

"Aren't we all, brother? You'll get by. Work it through." He shoved a file under my nose and a map that no longer resembled Austin for all the lines drawn across it. "Ready to work?"

I threw off my melancholy, determined to crack the solution I swore was right in front of my face. "Always."

Andy nodded his approval, and for a while we stopped speaking.

I didn't make it to the florist shop for another few days, snowed with work. Floss sent a few text messages, and I replied as best I could, but a wariness entered my tone and I couldn't help thinking that she knew what I was going to do. I pushed open the door, greeting Dolly, who sat on a freshly painted ledge in the morning sunshine.

"I'm in the back!" Floss called from the rear of the shop.

I let the door close behind me and pushed my way through the undergrowth. "There's more potted plants, and the bows are gone," I noted as I made my way to the desk. Several boxes were piled on top and I peered around them. "Do you want to carry these deliveries somewhere?"

"They're not mine." Floss appeared from behind orchid studded strands that separated the back office from the front shop area. "The driver is having a hard time working out where things go. She was fairly snarky this morning. Looks like someone might be playing a practical joke on her." She slipped out from behind the desk to wrap her arms around my waist, her head tipped back, parted lips inviting a kiss I desperately wanted to give her.

Blood rushed south, leaving the ground wobbling beneath my feet. "Ah. Floss. I was going to ask—"

"Do you need me for something?" she asked, undeterred by my lack of reaction. She rose onto her toes and I couldn't help myself from dipping my head to brush my lips over hers.

Nothing more. It's not fair to her.

My cock screamed obscenities in its confined space, but I ignored that too and sucked in a sharp breath. "I uh, don't need you for events or anything else. Anymore." the shop fell silent. I blew out the breath between my teeth. *Those weren't the words I practiced this morning.* "That— it came out wrong."

Floss dropped her arms to her sides and took a long step back, creating a cold abyss where her body warmth had been. "No. You said that just right. I'm fine with these boxes. Thanks." She turned her back to me in an obvious dismissal, the lines of her shoulders hard beneath the white stretchy shirt she wore over her jeans.

"Floss— I don't want to invalidate what we shared the other night." I stumbled over her name. *Just give up now and go. You can't fix this.*

But I wanted to. Badly.

"Yes you just have." Her words grounded me, brought me back.

I cleared my throat. "Why don't we start this again? Forget the fake stuff, and concentrate on—"

"Forget the fake stuff?" Her blue eyes flashed the color of a lightning struck sea, and like any doggone sailor, I held my ground. "I'm not sure there's anything real about you, Acton Cunningham. Why don't you go back to work and figure out who you're supposed to be and, in a few years, when you've grown the fuck up, you can come back and I'll see if you've made the mark. Not that it will be likely," she snapped.

I nodded slowly; I'd earned that one. "I'll leave you and Dolly alone. I'm sorry, Floss. It's for the best."

"Thank you for that." The words came out in the same tone she'd use for *get the fuck out.*

I backed up a step, trying to communicate the rent in my heart as I found the door with my ass. Swearing softly under my breath, I pulled the glassed door inward and a delivery man with arms stacked full of boxes stamped with the shop's logo fell in.

"Fuck. Sorry, man." I helped gather the parcels, dusting chalk off my hands along with some of the green spongy stuff cut flowers were always stuck into. "Sorry about the mess."

The man grumbled something in a language that sure as hell wasn't Texan, and headed toward the desk. I glanced over his shoulder but Floss had already hidden. My heart thumped dully in a hollow chest as I worked my way across the street, seeing nothing at all as I hit my office doors. In a short period I'd achieved the career upgrade I craved, found the perfect girl, fallen in love and broken her heart.

This was what I planned, what had been the right thing to do. So why did it feel so fucking bitten in my mouth?

Cursing softly and startling an old lady with a fluffy dog on a lead chattering to the reception desk, I hit the stairs, intent on running out my black mood.

How much fucking worse could today get?

CHAPTER EIGHT

FLOSS

I thanked the dark-haired man before me three times before I realized he was waiting on a signature from me.

"Sorry," I mumbled, barely glancing at the boxes stacked beside the desk. "There's no more, is there?"

"No," he answered in a thickly accented voice. "But I take these." He pointed to the first stack of deliveries that overpopulated the desk. "Take them back. Not for you."

"Ahhh," I started, glancing down at the register. Acton had thrown me totally off kilter and Ella only lasted an hour before she puked all over the office, which was currently airing even though she'd been gone for hours. There was a hole in my heart and my brain had stopped functioning. "I think I might check with the owner before you take anything, okay? I know there was a mix up but I don't want to send back anything she'd expected to be here."

"No. I take these. You sign." He thrust a digital pad into my hands.

I grabbed the brick of a device, clutching it tight. "It'll just take a moment." I set the brick down beside the register. "I'll call her."

"No." The driver—whom I realized I'd never met before—lunged forward, knocking my phone from my hand. It hit the tiled floor, a death-announcing crack echoing in my ears.

Today might be the worst day of my life.

I loved Acton, had just figured that out, and now he was gone. My phone was broken and the delivery driver was a psycho.

"Okay, that's enough." Biting back the urge to scream obscenities at the ceiling, I turned to him in full, my hands on my hips and came nose to barrel with a matte black handgun. Tiny scratches decorated the metal that was so close to my face I could see the depth of them. "Fu—"

"Those. Mine. I take."

"Hell yes." The words slipped out, and I nearly laughed as his eyes widened beyond the cannon stuck in my face. A giggle lodged in my throat and I doubled over, choking on a bout of hysterics.

This will not end well.

Already in a weird frame of mind, I disassociated from the entire situation, zooming back ass though I sat in the office, watching myself be threatened by a guy with dark hair and skin. Andy had given me a run down on how to memorize details in the event of a break in or hold up—the term had seemed so wild west that I laughed at him at the time. Now, my hysteria subsided into a cold dread, nothing seemed funny at all.

Remember all his details. Mark something on the wall that's the assailant's height. Eye color. Tatts. Shirt color. Shaved or not. Scars and markings. Everything helps.

"I'll get your boxes," I agreed, nodding like a bobblehead dog on a dashboard. I slipped my arms around the stack, trying to balance them all but they were way too heavy. "Ah, I'll take a few to the door, okay?"

I bumped my hip twice to the unmarked button beneath the desk, praying I hit the silent alarm all the way, unwilling to glance down and see if I'd got it. I grabbed the top two boxes and lugged them across the desk, making my load seem heavier than it was, keeping my steps tight. "We wondered about this, you know. The delivery girl was so confused."

"Don't talk." He motioned me toward the door.

I squeezed my eyes shut for an instant, and tried to remember how to breathe. More light steps, though I shouldn't have bothered. The gun pressed into my back as he cleared pots and displays with what sounded like his boot, the terracotta and ceramic vases splintering on the tiles.

My heart pounded in my head, filling it with a roar of white noise. My skin prickled cold. I reached the door and began to squat, wondering if this was a really bad idea. "I'll just put them here. You can take them and I'll get you the other one, okay?"

"Go outside." My companion didn't seem to be much for talking himself.

"Ah, that's not a good idea. People will scream if they see you with a gun."

I turned to face him in full, making sure not to stand in front of him so he was visible through the glass doors. Someone would have to be looking to see, but I prayed I'd done the right thing and someone—anyone—would be looking for exactly what I planned.

"No one will see. You go. I follow." He smiled, displaying yellowed teeth.

"That simple, huh?" I swallowed, unable to keep the fear off my face any longer.

He smiled wider, gesturing with his gun. "Go now."

I pivoted on my heel to face the glass doors and had my second shock in less than five minutes. Acton stood on the other side of the door, his weapon drawn while I stood between the two men. He mouthed *down*, and I dropped like a stone, my hands already covering my head as I dropped the boxes on the floor. The door slammed open, narrowly missing me in its wide arc and a single shot fired.

Something heavy fell behind me, hitting the floor with a muted thud.

Someone.

Bile rose in my throat. It looked like Ella wasn't the only one who would be vomiting in the shop today.

I stayed in my crouch, staying at the tiled floor that fluctuated beneath me until warm, familiar hands gripped my arms and wound around me. I pressed my lips to the front of Acton's shirt, over his heart. A large hand clasped the back of my head, pulling me into his body in full.

"I'm so sorry, Floss. God, girl. I'm sorry. I shouldn't have left you or said anything at all. Christ, girl. Tell me you're okay." He bent in front of me, staring into my face while I hiccuped and tried not to throw up on him.

"You killed him." There hadn't been a single sound behind me. Not a groan or anything. Acton was that damn good at his job and, fight or not, I was so glad he'd answered the call. Because the shop's silent alarm, unlike the one in a normal shop, didn't go off in the local police station. It alerted the Rangers office across the street.

"Did he hurt you?" Acton glared over my shoulder, the look in his eyes telling me he'd like to bring the dead man back to life and shoot him all over again.

"You killed someone."

"It's my job, Floss." He checked me over while I stood still and let him. What was the point in moving? Voices and other bodies filled the shop but I didn't take any notice. The only person who meant anything stood right in front of me. "I shouldn't have left you. Fuck." He wrapped me in his arms and I let him, clenching my fists in his shirt as I began to shake. "You did good. Real good."

"I wanted to punch him. And I wanted to wet myself. I dunno. I might have."

Acton laughed and groped my ass. "Nope, all good." His heart beat a little faster in his chest, a little louder and I knew it wasn't only me who had been scared.

I tiled my head back, my heart in my throat as I looked at him. "I—"

He pressed two fingers to my mouth. "Fight me later, Floss. Right now I need to sit down and talk to you before this all flies out of your mind."

"That's not likely," I spoke around his fingers. "And I'm not fighting with you. I love you."

Acton held me at a small distance, watching me carefully. "I know. I love you too."

His figure blurred as my eyes filled with salt. "If you knew, why did you— say what you did?" *Is this really important right now? There's a dead man on my floor.*

"Cunningham." Andy's familiar voice broke into our conversation. "You need to see this."

Acton leaned down and slowly and very deliberately kissed my mouth. "Come with me?"

My heartrate picked up. I nodded blindly, the tears spilling forth to cascade over my cheeks, uncaring who saw. Those words were loaded with meaning and I followed him to where Andy knelt, Ella's delivery boxes torn open.

White power filtered out of it, and when Andy gestured toward the stack I dropped earlier, tiny sachets of pink and white pills tumbled to the floor.

"Your drugs," I murmured, staring at them. "How— weren't they picked up at a different, I don't know, level?"

"Should have been." Andy was already on the phone— to Ella, I assumed.

"Tell her I'll clean up after. She doesn't have to come in," I called.

Andy threw me a thumbs up, but I could already hear Ella's squark from the other end of the line.

"I'll help but we could be here all day. Process." Acton sent me a lopsided grin. His fingers folded around mine. "I was so damn scared knowing you were down here alone."

"You mean it?" I blinked, his words still turning over in my brain. "What you said before…why, Acton? I—that really hurt," I whispered.

He nodded somberly, gathering me into his arms, and I let him. "I hurt bad, too. Knew straightaway I made the wrong choice and fucked it up. But I didn't think you wanted to see me again."

"I was fairly pissed," I admitted. Someone draped a blanket around my shoulders, and Acton gathered that into his arms too, creating a barrier between us and the rest of the world. "But I'm glad you came. I was trying to stall. I sucked at it. And I tried to remember all the things Andy told me about hold ups. It seemed so silly at the time."

Acton glanced over his shoulder and back to me. "No so silly now, huh? How about we go into the back office? You talk, I'll listen. About this. Us. Whatever you want. I won't go unless you tell me." He raised an eyebrow to make it a question.

I nodded. "Okay, but I gotta warn you, the office smells like puke. Ella," I added.

He grimaced. "How abouts you pick somewhere, and same deal. Good?"

"That sounds good," I whispered, energy draining from me as he kissed the top of my head, then my nose, then my lips. "But only if it's all one hundred percent real from here on in. Everything, no matter how much it hurts or how scared we are. Deal?"

Acton smiled against my lips, kissing me gently. "Deal," he whispered.

I hope you loved Acton and Floss' whirlwind romance. Their story leads into my Texan Devils series, which starts with Andy and Ella's second chance romance in RANGER'S WISH.

Bear gets his own story in RANGER'S FURY.

ABOUT THE AUTHOR

USA Today Bestselling author Sofia Aves writes fast-paced police romances, sizzling military units, steamy cowboys with a Montana backdrop and the occasional cheeky god. Married to a veteran, she often tackles topics of PTSD and reintegration and has a soft spot for all who work in uniform. Sofia writes kidlit for charity and has over one hundred and fifty publications including translations into five languages across four not-so-super-secret pen names.

Sofia is a mum of three crazies in a returned veteran household and has an overly large fur baby who thinks she's a teacup puppy. After eighteen years of planning and dreaming, Sofia and her husband opened Lorendel Alpaca Park with their first starter herd.

Sofia lives near Brisbane, Australia.

Sign up to Sofia's newsletter and get a free Blue Blooded Brothers book.

Haven't read the Z Boy's prequel? Get it for free here:

A TABLE FOR TEN

www.sofiaves.com

Follow Sofia on

BookBub

Twitter

Instagram

Read Sofia's Series

Blue Blooded Brothers

Red Hart Ranch

Texan Devils

Z BOYS

Australian Customs Security

SUNDAE DREAMING

Christmas Romance

Shortbread Shakedown

Klauss Brothers

Paranormal Romance

Trickster's Law

A Portrait in Ash & Lace

Complete WILD BLOOMS Series

Don't forget to leave a review for your favorite books

Snapdragons and Seductions - Sofia Aves

Saffron and Secrets - Sharon Woods

Blossom and Bliss - L.A. Shaw

Willows and Waterlilies - Taylor K Scott

Roses and Redemption - Denise T Ford

Wildflowers and Whispers - Maci Dillon

Bluebonnets and Bikers - D. Lilac

Magnolias and Memories - T M Caruso

Lavender and Lust - Jacyln Combe

Jasmine and Jealousy - Rhiannon Marina

Tulips and Truths - Mila Chase

Lilacs and Lovers - J R Gale

Chrysanthemum and Smolder - V L Peters

Lotus and Longing - LaLa Montgomery

Daisies and Desire - Ann Penny

Sunflowers and Surrender - L M Fox

Forget-me-nots and Fireworks - Elle Nicoll

Peonies and Promises - Lizzie Moreton

Heather and Heartache - VR Tennent

All books are available in eBook and paperback.